Happy Birthday to You, You Belong in a Zoo

Diane de Groat

HarperCollinsPublishers

Watercolors were used for the full-color illustrations.
The text type is 14-point Korinna.

Copyright © 1999 by Diane deGroat

Manufactured in China.
Library of Congress Cataloging-in-Publication Data
DeGroat, Diane.
Happy birthday to you, you belong in a zoo / Diane deGroat.
p. cm.
Summary: Before Lewis's birthday party, Gilbert's mother
wisely substitutes a toy for the frying pan Gilbert wants to give Lewis.
ISBN-10: 0-06-001029-0 (pbk.) — ISBN-13: 978-0-06-001029-4 (pbk.)
ISBN-10: 0-688-16545-1 (lib. bdg.) — ISBN-13: 978-0-688-16545-1 (lib. bdg.)
[1. Gifts—Fiction.   2. Birthdays—Fiction.   3. Parties—Fiction.
4. Schools—Fiction.   5. Friendship—Fiction.]   I. Title.
PZ7.D3639Hap   1999   [E]—dc21   98-44722   CIP   AC

♪ ...Happy Birthday, dear Janice...
♪ Happy Birthday to you... ♪♪

"I got mail!" Gilbert shouted. He waved a blue envelope over his head. "See?" he said. "It has my name on it!"

Father put down his shopping list and had a look. "G, I, L, B, E, R, T," he spelled. "Why, it *is* for you, Gilbert. Who sent it?"

Gilbert pulled out the card. It had a picture of a cake and candles on the front. Inside it said:

COME TO A BIRTHDAY PARTY

FOR   LEWIS

ON   SATURDAY

AT   3:00

P.S. Bring a present

"That sounds like fun," Father said.

But Gilbert made a face. "No it doesn't. Lewis isn't my friend. I don't want to go to his party, and I don't want to give him a present."

Mother said, "Lewis wants you to be there, Gilbert. That sounds like something a friend would ask."

Gilbert thought about that. Maybe Lewis really did want Gilbert to be his friend. Maybe Lewis would be nice to Gilbert at the party, and not tease him like he did in school.

"You'll have a good time," Mother said. "And we can shop for a present after school tomorrow."

When Gilbert got to school the next morning, he saw Lewis on the playground, playing catch with Frank. Now that Gilbert was Lewis's friend, he could play catch, too.

He ran over and asked, "Can I play?"

"Later," Lewis said.

But the bell rang before Gilbert could play, and everyone had to go inside.

At lunch, Gilbert tried to sit next to Lewis, but Lewis wouldn't move over to make room. Gilbert sat next to Patty instead.

"I thought you didn't like Lewis," Patty said.

"He's my friend now," Gilbert answered. "He wants me to come to his party on Saturday."

"I wasn't invited," Patty said. "I guess I'm not his friend."

At recess, Mrs. Byrd passed out jump ropes and rubber balls, but they were all taken by the time Gilbert and Patty got there. "Wait here," Gilbert said to Patty. "I'll ask my friend Lewis if we can play ball with him."

Gilbert waved and called to Lewis, but Lewis didn't hear him because there was so much noise. Gilbert had to shout, "Can we play, too?"

"No," Lewis shouted back.

"Why not?" Gilbert asked.

"We have too many players already," Lewis said.

"Oh," Gilbert said.

Gilbert followed Lewis onto the ball field and said, "Thanks for inviting me to your party."

"What?" Lewis said.

Gilbert yelled into Lewis's ear, "I SAID I'M COMING TO YOUR PARTY ON SATURDAY."

Lewis caught the ball and threw it to home plate. The bell rang, and recess was over. He turned to Gilbert and said, "My mother made me invite all the boys in the class. That's why you got an invitation. And you better bring me a present, too, if you want any cake and ice cream."

After school, Mother took Gilbert to the Big Mart to shop for the party. Gilbert knew he had to bring a present, because he wanted cake and ice cream, but he didn't really want to give Lewis anything except maybe a smelly old shoe.

They walked up and down the toy aisle. Mother picked up a glow-in-the-dark kick ball. "Look, Gilbert," she said. "Does Lewis like to play ball?"

Gilbert said, "Lewis doesn't like to play ball. He hates it. He would be very upset if I gave him a ball."

Mother said, "Hmmm. I see."

Then Mother picked up a new toy that Gilbert hadn't seen before. "Do you think Lewis would like this, Gilbert?"

It was a Martian Spaceship, and it was the perfect size for Gilbert's Martian Space Pilot action figures. When he pushed the buttons, it made rocket noises.

"I like it," Gilbert announced. "I want it for me."

Mother said, "We'll get one to put away for your birthday next month. But you can't have it until then. And we can get one for Lewis, too."

But Gilbert said, "Lewis will hate that. He will be very upset if I give him a Martian Spaceship."

"Hmmm. I see," Mother said. "And what *would* Lewis like for his birthday?"

The housewares section was at the end of the toy
aisle. Gilbert walked over and picked up a frying pan.
"Here is a nice present," he said.

"Are you sure?" Mother asked.

"Yes," Gilbert answered. "This is perfect. I want to give this to Lewis."

"You are absolutely sure," Mother repeated.

"Very absolutely," Gilbert said, dropping the pan into the cart.

And all the way home he sang, "Happy birthday to you.... You belong in a zoo.... You look like a monkey... and you smell like one, too."

On Saturday, Gilbert rang Lewis's doorbell, trying hard not to drop the present. His mother had wrapped it in bright paper and ribbons, and Gilbert couldn't wait to see Lewis's face when he opened it.

Lewis answered the door. "It's about time," he said. "Come on. We're playing musical chairs and we need one more person."

All the boys from Mrs. Byrd's class were inside, and they started running around the chairs as soon as the music started. Lewis was the first one out. "No fair," he whined. "It's my birthday!"

The game continued until only Gilbert and Kenny were left. When the music stopped, Gilbert got the seat and Kenny sat down right on top of him. Gilbert was squished, but he had won the game! Lewis handed him a prize. It was a Martian Space Pilot action figure—one that Gilbert didn't have!

After the games, it was time for cake and ice cream. Gilbert's stomach began to hurt when he remembered his present. He wasn't mad at Lewis anymore. He hoped that everyone would go home before Lewis opened his gifts. But Lewis suddenly jumped from the table and shouted, "Presents!"

The boys sat in a circle around the gifts, and Lewis
opened them up one by one. There were video games,
a truck, and a glow-in-the-dark kick ball. Gilbert kept
an eye on the door, hoping his mother would come to
pick him up.

When there was one present left, Gilbert felt like he
was going to wet his pants.

"This one's from Gilbert," Lewis announced, holding
up the brightly wrapped package. "And boy, is it heavy."

Gilbert didn't know what he was going to do. Maybe he
could say that his mother gave him the wrong gift, and
that he would bring the right one to school on Monday.
He closed his eyes and waited for Lewis to say something.

Lewis did say something. He said, "Wow! Thanks, Gilbert!"

Gilbert opened his eyes and saw Lewis holding up
a brand-new Martian Spaceship with flashing lights
and rocket noises.

Gilbert was very quiet when his mother came
to pick him up.

"How was the party?" she finally asked him
as they walked home.

"Fine."

"Did you have a good time?"

"Yes."

"Did you have cake and ice cream?"

"Yes."

"Did Lewis like your present?"

"Yes."

When they got home, Father was busy cooking. "This new frying pan is great!" he said. "Would you like some apple pancakes, Gilbert?"

Gilbert was about to say that he wasn't hungry when Mother said, "Oh, my. That frying pan looks like Lewis's birthday present. I must have given you the wrong gift, Gilbert. I hope Lewis was not too upset when he got a spaceship instead of a frying pan."

Gilbert smiled and said, "No, it was the perfect gift." He gave Mother a hug.

Then he ate three large apple pancakes
with maple syrup.